The Tuttle Story: "Books to Span the East and West"

Most people are surprised to learn that the world's largest publisher of books on Asia had its humble beginnings in the tiny American state of Vermont. The company's founder, Charles E. Tuttle, belonged to a New England family steeped in publishing. And his first love was naturally books—especially old and rare editions.

Immediately after WW II, serving in Tokyo under General Douglas MacArthur, Tuttle was tasked with reviving the Japanese publishing industry. He later founded the Charles E. Tuttle Publishing Company, which thrives today as one of the world's leading independent publishers.

Though a westerner, Tuttle was hugely instrumental in bringing a knowledge of Japan and Asia to a world hungry for information about the East. By the time of his death in 1993, Tuttle had published over 6,000 books on Asian culture, history and art—a legacy honored by the Japanese emperor with the "Order of the Sacred Treasure," the highest tribute Japan can bestow upon a non-Japanese.

With a backlist of 1,500 titles, Tuttle Publishing is more active today than at any time in its past—inspired by Charles Tuttle's core mission to publish fine books to span the East and West and provide a greater understanding of each.

Published by Tuttle Publishing, an imprint of Periplus Editions (HK) Ltd.

www.tuttlepublishing.com

Copyright © 2012 John Stickler and Soma Han

Library of Congress Cataloging-in-Publication Data
Han, Soma.
 Maya and the turtle : a Korean fairy tale / by Soma Han and John C. Stickler ; illustrated by Soma Han. -- 1st ed.
   p. cm.
  ISBN 978-0-8048-4277-8 (hardback)
[1. Fairy tales. 2. Korea--Fiction.] I. Stickler, John. II. Title.
 PZ8.S645May 2012
 [Fic]--dc23
            2011052443

ISBN 978-0-8048-4277-8

First edition
16 15 14 13 12   6 5 4 3 2 1   1205EP
Printed in Hong Kong

Distributed by

North America, Latin America & Europe
Tuttle Publishing
364 Innovation Drive
North Clarendon, VT 05759-9436 U.S.A.
Tel: 1 (802) 773-8930
Fax: 1 (802) 773-6993
info@tuttlepublishing.com
www.tuttlepublishing.com

Japan
Tuttle Publishing
Yaekari Building, 3rd Floor
5-4-12 Osaki, Shinagawa-ku Tokyo 141 0032
Tel: (81) 3 5437-0171
Fax: (81) 3 5437-0755
sales@tuttle.co.jp
www.tuttle.co.jp

Asia Pacific
Berkeley Books Pte. Ltd.
61 Tai Seng Avenue #02-12
Singapore 534167
Tel: (65) 6280-1330
Fax: (65) 6280-6290
inquiries@periplus.com.sg
www.periplus.com

TUTTLE PUBLISHING® is a registered trademark of Tuttle Publishing, a division of Periplus Editions (HK) Ltd.

Maya
and
the
Turtle

SOMA HAN and JOHN C. STICKLER
illustrated by SOMA HAN

TUTTLE Publishing

Tokyo | Rutland, Vermont | Singapore

Long, long ago, in a small village in a far away land, there lived a young girl named Maya. She and her father lived in a small house with a roof made of rice straw. Her father was a poet and a scholar. They were poor but very proud.

When Maya was a little girl, her mother died. On her deathbed* she had called Maya to her side and told her a story.

* Many Koreans sleep on the floor. The mattress (*yo*) and comforter (*ibul*) are folded and put away during the day.

"My child," she said in a weak voice, "listen carefully. When you grow up you will become a princess. I know this because of a *temong* dream* I had before you were born. A *temong* dream is a prophecy; they always come true. I dreamed a bright star came down from heaven and I held it with both hands. Therefore, you must take care of yourself and look after your father. You will not see me any more, but remember, my spirit will always watch over you."

Maya and her father were very sad. Even the sky wept for them. But life went on. Her father did everything he could to make Maya grow up happy and healthy. And she did, growing more beautiful every year, and very wise for her age.

Oh my little one, little one do not cry.
Your mama will return when a kitty cat grows horns on his head.

* A woman expecting a baby might have the special kind of dream known as the *temong* dream. It is said that a *temong* dream is a magical look into the child's future

One glorious spring day Maya was walking through the fields, picking flowers and wild vegetables. The birds sang and the fields were covered with bright, new flowers, popping joyously from the ground after the long, cold winter. The earth was rejoicing in its symphony of spring.

Maya stopped by her favorite rock. Legend said that this rock was magic, and that if you whispered a wish here it would come true. Every day Maya came here to make a wish. To her surprise, she found a baby turtle* on top of the rock.

* In Korea turtles are a symbol of long life. There are many kinds of turtles, and some can live to be well over 100!

"Hello, little one," Maya said. "How did you get up there? Have you lost your mother? I will take care of you. I don't have a mother either." And she gently picked him up and took him home. She put the little turtle down in the flower garden and he was very happy. She named him Boke-doongi.*

Each day Boke-doongi would appear at the door to the kitchen and Maya would give him something to eat. Even when there was very little food for Maya and her father, she always saved something for him.

Boke-doongi grew bigger and bigger each year, and whenever Maya went into the countryside to pick berries or herbs he would follow slowly behind her.

---

* *Boke-doongi* in Korean means "lucky one."

One winter Maya's father became ill and could not work. There was no money for medicine or even for food. Maya tried to think of a way to make some money, but the fields were covered with snow and she could not even gather wild berries or herbs.

She knew of a prosperous village on the other side of the mountain. That village was cursed by a monstrous centipede. It would fly* into the village on cold winter nights when the moon was full, attacking the village children. The people lived in terror. Finally, they said, "Maybe if we sacrifice one person, the centipede will leave us alone."

And so a tradition began. Once a year, they would buy a young girl for the centipede and leave her outside the village. The next morning, the girl would be gone forever, but the village would be safe for one more year.

Maya decided that to help her father get well again, she would volunteer to face the giant centipede. The villagers paid a great deal of money to anyone brave enough to become a midnight sacrifice.

* Real centipedes don't fly. The one in this story was a magical monster.

One chilly fall day, Maya secretly hiked over the mountain to the other village. The sky was heavy with ominous clouds. The villagers welcomed her and were grateful that she was willing to meet the horrible centipede.

"Thank you," they said, and held a ceremony under the *chungja* tree.* The *chungja* tree was a special gathering place for picnics and ceremonies near the totem poles** which guarded the village entrance. At the ceremony, the village elders blessed Maya's soul and prayed for the safety of their village. Then they gave her the money.

---

* *Chungja* means "shelter" and a *chungja* tree is usually a large, shady tree along the rural road where people naturally stop to rest, step out of the sun or rain, or perhaps enjoy the view

** Many villages posted carved wooden totem pole guardians (*changsung*), male and female figures to keep away evil spirits.

Maya bought the medicine her father needed and enough food and clothing for a year. She nurtured him and watched him recover his health. Soon he was strong and able to care for himself again.

Finally, the dreaded night came, the night of the January full moon. Maya prepared her father's favorite meal and served him for the last time. She knew she would never see him again.

And so she kissed him good night and crept out of the little house. Boke-doongi followed slowly behind her until she turned to him.

"Please don't follow me, dear one," she said, giving him a kiss. "I love you, but you must stay home and look after Father, for I am not coming back." And she ran up the hill so Boke-doongi could not follow her.

Instead of a table and chairs, people in Korean homes sat on flat floor cushions and ate at a low table that could be carried from the kitchen, all set with food, plates and chopsticks.

The floor Maya and her father are sitting on is warm. This is because the heat from the kitchen fireplace flows through pipes under the floors before it reaches a chimney on the other side of the house. This heating system is called *ondol* and has been used in Korea for thousands of years.

The night was deathly silent, so quiet it seemed even the earth and the sky were afraid to breathe. The cold, bright moon lighted the path over the mountain and cast dark shadows under the leafless trees. To Maya they looked like tall, black monsters reaching out to grab her. She shivered with cold and fear.

When Maya reached the cursed place, she dropped to her knees, wrapped herself in her blanket, and waited for her destiny. Sadly, she remembered her mother's last words, "You will become a princess," and, "My spirit will watch over you always."

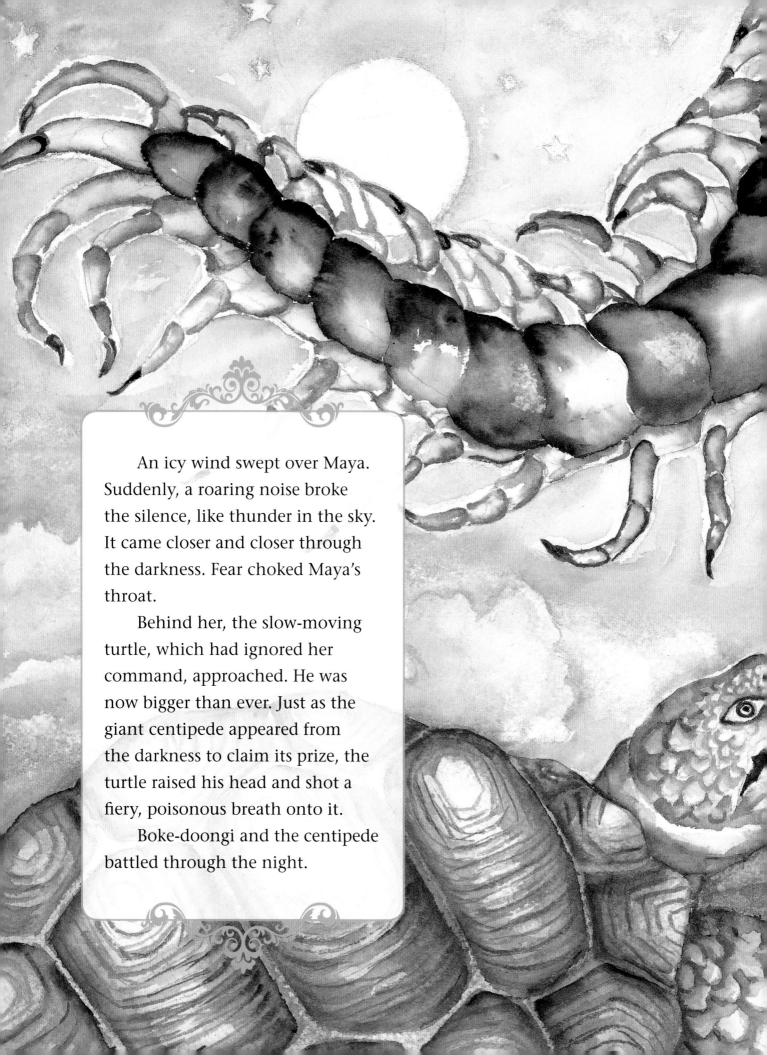

An icy wind swept over Maya. Suddenly, a roaring noise broke the silence, like thunder in the sky. It came closer and closer through the darkness. Fear choked Maya's throat.

Behind her, the slow-moving turtle, which had ignored her command, approached. He was now bigger than ever. Just as the giant centipede appeared from the darkness to claim its prize, the turtle raised his head and shot a fiery, poisonous breath onto it.

Boke-doongi and the centipede battled through the night.

The next morning the villagers approached carefully and quietly. During the night a light snow had fallen. They were surprised to find Maya, nearly frozen, next to the dead bodies of the giant centipede and the big turtle.

"The monster centipede is dead!" the villagers cried. "The turtle saved her life!" The village was safe forever, and the villagers threw a great feast. "She offered her life to save her father," they said, and shook their heads in wonder. Then they sang and danced for joy.*

* The two dancers at the lower left are wearing carved wooden masks for the Mask Dance, like a life-size puppet show with music.

News of the courageous girl spread quickly around the world. Soon, the story reached the Emperor of heaven and earth.*

"I must reward this young woman," he said, and ordered servants to take silk, jewels and wonderful gifts to her little house in the country. "Invite them to the palace," he instructed.

The Emperor prepared a beautiful house in the clouds for Maya and her father to live in. When they arrived, he told Maya, "You must meet my son, the Prince, when he returns from his journey."

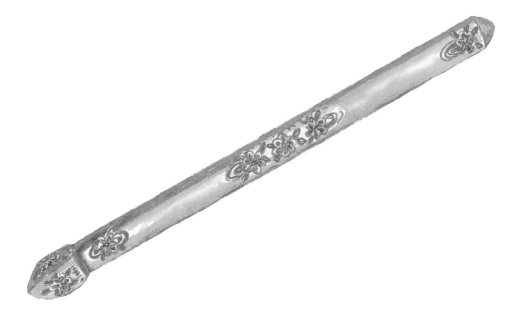

* Long ago, the Koreans and other Asian peoples believed that their emperor was divine, although he did not live up in the clouds, the way this story's Emperor of Heaven and Earth does.

Maya looked forward to the day she would meet the Prince, and spent the time sewing her happy songs into the beautiful silk dresses she made. She wrote a poem,* as her father had taught her to do.

The cold moon sees all:
The tortoise and the maiden.
In spring, life returns.

---

* Maya's poem is a Japanese form of verse called a Haiku.
  It is related to a longer type of poem from Korea, called Sijo.

The day finally came when the Prince arrived from his travels in far away lands. He rode on a strange beast* Maya had never seen before. When they met, it was love at first sight.

---

* Why is the Prince riding on a dinosaur? "They are very strong," the Prince says, "and can walk long distances without getting tired."

Very soon the Prince asked Maya to become his bride. The Emperor was happy that his wandering son had decided to marry such a wonderful girl. He said to himself, "This is a marriage made in heaven."

The Emperor commanded that a royal wedding be held at the palace and invitations were sent out around the world. The wedding celebration went on for days, attended by people from many lands.

After the wedding, the Emperor gave the happy couple a beautiful land, a natural paradise to live on and rule in peace.

They lived there happily ever after.

The symbols surrounding my mother are letters of the Korean alphabet, which is called Hangeul

Author's Note

My mother, T. M. Song, was a storyteller, and *Maya and the Turtle* is a tale she used to tell me when I was a little girl. Her mother had told it to her when she was growing up in a small village in Korea. Whenever my mother reached the story's end she would say, "And that was the beginning of their dynasty."

My mother was born in 1900, during the reign of King Kojong, Korea's last monarch. She was a direct descendant of Song Si Yul who served in the royal court. This book is dedicated to her memory.